WHY THE ROPE WENT TIGHT

Words by
Bamber Gascoigne
Pictures by
Christina Gascoigne

LOTHROP, LEE & SHEPARD BOOKS
New York

"Hold one end of this rope for me," the clown said.
"Just for a moment. There's a good lad."

Mike was outside the big top,
waiting to see the circus.
And he did what the clown said.
He held one end of the rope.

And suddenly the rope went tight.

Why the rope went tight was . . .

because just round the corner was Frank the Furter,

who had sold the World's
Longest Frankfurter to Mike's friend Millie,
who had been given the other end of the rope by the clown.
"Hold this," the clown had said, "just for a moment, there's a
good lass." Millie was just taking her first bite,

when suddenly she was pulled off her feet because . . .

a greedy brown
dog called Pedigree
Chump had grabbed the

end of the World's
Longest Frankfurter
but his lead went tight
and squashed his owner Spruce Bruce
flat as a sardine against Saucy Sal,
with whom he was enjoying a quick kiss and cuddle,

while Saucy Sal was being pulled the other way . . .

by her own
Spotted Shrimp,
a horrible hound
who had sunk his teeth

deep in the star-studded
backside of Sorro, the
World's Greatest Ladder-Gadder,
who lost his balance

and down came his end of the ladder . . .

upsetting the
Seven Tooty Frooties as
well as Barrel-Bottomed Ben,
and as the Seventh Tooty Frooty
came tumbling down,

she grabbed at a tape measure with which . . .

Glob the Blob,
Fattest Known Man,
was being measured
for trousers by the Mighty Atom,
Smallest Dwarf in Five Continents,
and as the tape went tight,

the Mighty Atom grabbed at a lever . . .

which started
a steam engine
that was used
for pulling in
the ropes of the

big top, and as the drum began to turn
it caught just a few of the hairs of the beard
of the World's Hairiest Lady, and it might have
done her a bit of damage, but the tip of the tail
of a snake was tight round her toes

because she had been talking to . . .

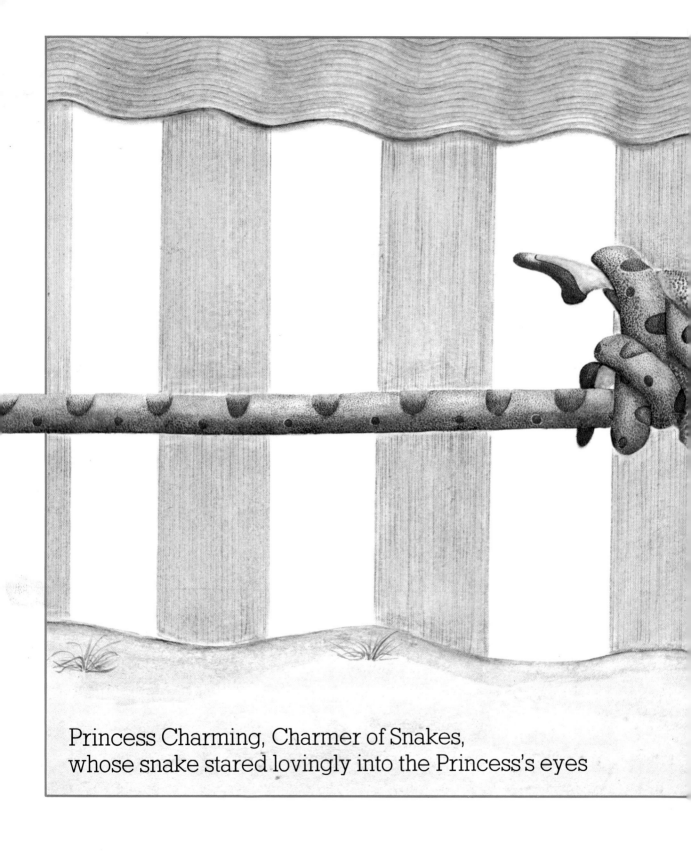

Princess Charming, Charmer of Snakes,
whose snake stared lovingly into the Princess's eyes

but the Princess had eyes only for
the man whose magnificent moustache

she had been gently stroking . . .

Mr.
Muscle
Himself,
Strongest Man in the Universe, who felt a slight tug at

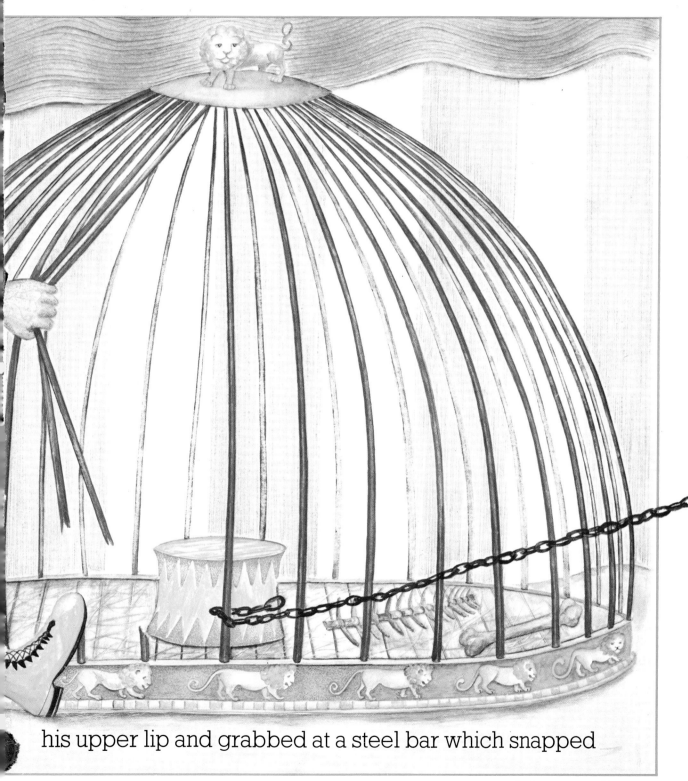

his upper lip and grabbed at a steel bar which snapped

and out of the gap leapt . . .

Lickchop Leo,
the fiercest, greediest,
and most generally rumptious and
bumptious lion that Creation has ever known
(which is why his keeper always kept him chained).

And that was why the rope went tight.
And it also went tight because it wasn't any longer than it was,

which was lucky for Mike and . . .

for Mike's friend Millie
and Frank the Furter
and Pedigree Chump
and Spruce Bruce and Saucy Sal
not to mention Spotted Shrimp
and Sorro and the Tooty Frooties
with Barrel-Bottomed Ben
and Glob the Blob
and the Mighty Atom
and the World's Hairiest Lady
and Princess Charming and the Snake
and even for Mr. Muscle Himself.

Very lucky indeed!

And the moral of
this story is:
If some clown asks you
to hold a piece of rope,
always make sure you
know what is at
the other end.